TEDDY TALKS

A Paws-itive story about Type 1 Diabetes

By Vanessa Messenger

Edited by Nadara "Nay" Merrill
Photography by Mioara Dragan

FIRST EDITION

ISBN 978-1-7369997-0-7 (Hardcover)

ISBN 978-1-7369997-1-4 (Softcover)

www.messengerpublishingbooks.com

messenger ✈
PUBLISHING

For Jeff, Monroe, Baby Messenger (and of course, Teddy!)
who motivate me every day with their love and support
behind everything I do. To the Priebe, Kolp, Endres families,
and beloved Grandma Zerilli for guiding and encouraging me
with unconditional love. - Vanessa

To Grandma and Grandpa for always showering me (and my
Humans!) with lots of love, care, and long car rides! - Teddy

Teddy's T1D Terms
Let's learn some new words together!

Type 1 Diabetic (T1D): Someone, like my human Emily, whose body does not make insulin. Your body needs insulin in order to use the food you eat for energy. You need energy to do everyday activities.

Insulin: Insulin turns your food into energy. When a diabetic does not make insulin on their own, they may take a medication that will help their body turn food into energy.

Energy: Is what your body needs to do fun activities like running, playing, and learning.

Sugar Levels (Glucose/Blood Sugar Levels): Throughout the day, the amount of sugar in Emily's body goes up and down depending on what we eat, when we eat and the activities we do.

Monitor: A cool machine that measures how much sugar is in the body at any point in time.

Target Range: A set of numbers (a small number and a big number) Emily tries to keep her sugar levels in between so they are not too low or too high. Emily's doctor tells her what the best range is for her body.

Supplies: Different items a Type 1 Diabetic might need to keep them healthy such as insulin medicine, needles, a glucose monitor, and sugary snacks. Emily's doctor helps her make a list of all the supplies she might need.

I know every dog probably says this, but my human, Emily, is a very good girl. She is also a T1D, which is our nickname for being a Type 1 Diabetic.

Type 1 Diabetes means her body does not make insulin on its own. Insulin allows the body to use the sugar from food and turn it into energy. Without it, food would stay as sugar and build up in parts of the body instead of being used as fuel to do fun things like run in the backyard or play hide-and-seek.

Emily takes insulin medicine to keep her sugar levels normal so she has energy to do all her favorite activities with me.

Whenever I take medicine, Mom and Dad have to hide it in peanut butter, but Emily takes hers all on her own!

Throughout the day, Emily's sugar levels in her body change depending on what she eats, when she eats, or how much we play. To keep track of her levels, Emily gets to carry around a cool monitor that makes different sounds depending on her sugars being high or low.

I do not get to have a cool monitor like Emily because I am not a T1D. Instead, I bring my squeaky toy everywhere so I can make noises too!

We like to show her monitor to the
other tiny humans in the neighborhood -
they think it is awesome!

I try to show them my squeaky toy, but they throw it
and I have to keep running after it!

The monitor shows a number to let us know how much sugar is in her body.

We call them "scores" like in a game!

Emily aims to keep the scores in her target range so they are not too high or to

low - and I help!

take Emily for walks...

Eat healthy foods that fall off her plate...

Exercise with her in the living room...

Make sure she has all her supplies before she leaves the house...

And spin around really fast until I catch my tail!

I am not sure if this part helps Emily with her scores, but it makes her laugh, and I love making her happy!

Emily's monitor makes a loud *BEEP* sound when she has a low score - that is when Mom and Dad give her a small sugar snack.

I tried to share one of my puppy treats with her once, but Mom said a small piece of candy or juice is better.

Her monitor makes a big *BUZZ* sound when her scores are too high - that means she needs some insulin medicine.

It is also time for me to give her lots of snuggles
until her scores are in good range again.

I am *really* good at this part!

Sometimes after dinner, Mom gives Emily and me dessert. But before we can have our treats, we each have to do a trick!

For Emily's trick, she gives herself insulin medicine so she can eat her treat without her score getting too high.

Before I get to eat my treat, everyone always makes me show them how to roll over. I wonder why they keep forgetting how to roll?!

Emily has to poke herself sometimes to check her scores or when she needs medicine, but she is so brave she says it does not even hurt!

he is the strongest person I know, and when I need a shot at the veterinarian, I think of her and then I feel strong too.

At first, Emily did not think it was very fun to check her scores. But now, it is part of our routine together.

In a lot of ways, I think Emily is even healthier than most humans because she makes good choices to eat well and be active every day!

Taking care of ourselves helps Emily get more scores in her target range...

... so we can have fun adventures together, just like everybody else!

The healthy choices we make while Emily is a tiny human will support her as she grows to be a big human like Mom. Or, an even *bigger* human like Grandma!

And I get to help her every day as she gets older.

Lucky for me, that is a VERY long time... especially in dog years!

About the Author

Vanessa Messenger is a Mom, a Product Lead at Google, and considering she's been a Type 1 Diabetic since 2010, she's also full-time pancreas!

With her background in Psychology and Broadcast Communications, she's always been impassioned by creating a connection with people through Storytelling. After receiving so much support and encouragement from the deep-rooted community of "diabuddies," she was determined to help create that same sense of belonging and connection for T1D kids through *Teddy Talks*.

A Note from Teddy

When my human, Vanessa, told me she wanted to write a book about me, I was so excited (cue the pup-arazzi!). Even though I'm not a certified Diabetic alert dog, I've learned a lot of *in-fu-mation* about Type 1 Diabetes from Vanessa and her doctor. I may be just a regular "Teddy Bear" Pomeranian who enjoys peanut butter and car rides, but I like to think I also have a special gift for making people smile! To connect with me and see more of my adorable personality, follow me on TikTok and Instagram @TeddyTheT1Dog.

CPSIA information can be obtained
at www.ICGtesting.com
Printed in the USA
LVHW071819180222
711490LV00009B/220